Quentin Blake

ANGELICA SPROCKET'S POCKETS

RED FOX

For l'équipe QB,
with love and thanks

Angelica Sprocket lives next door.
Her overcoat has pockets galore.

There's a pocket
for mice,

and a pocket
for cheese

and a pocket for hankies
in case anyone feels that they're
going to sneeze.

There's a pocket for all kinds of umbrellas

for when it begins to rain.

And another one with
swimming costumes and towels

for when the sun
comes out again.

There's a pocket for ducks,
and a pocket
for boats

and a pocket with lovely straw hats

for GOATS.

And in case anyone is thinking
of dropping off to sleep,
there's a pocket for

motorhorns that go PAH-HEE-

HAR-HUR and BEEP-BEEP.

There's a pocket for skateboards
(just look at those
skaters!)

and another pocket for

ALLIGATORS.

There's a pocket for ice cream
and all kinds of nice things
to drink.

There's a pocket for
   saucepans and frying pans and buckets

and spoons and forks and cheesegraters and

the kitchen SINK.

There's a

pocket for an

ELEPHANT, green and pink,

and another pocket for...

WHAT DO
YOU THINK?

There's more and more
and more
and more.
Angelica Sprocket has pockets galore!

Some other books by Quentin Blake

All Join In
Angel Pavement
Angelo
Clown
Cockatoos
Daddy Lost His Head
(Written by André Bouchard)
Fantastic Daisy Artichoke
The Green Ship
Mister Magnolia
Mrs Armitage and the Big Wave
Mrs Armitage on Wheels
Mrs Armitage Queen of the Road
Patrick
Quentin Blake's ABC
A Sailing Boat in the Sky
Simpkin
Snuff
Zagazoo

ANGELICA SPROCKET'S POCKETS
A RED FOX BOOK 978 1 862 30969 2

First published in Great Britain by Jonathan Cape,
an imprint of Random House Children's Books
A Random House Group Company

Jonathan Cape edition published 2010
Red Fox edition published 2011

1 3 5 7 9 10 8 6 4 2

Red Fox Books are published by Random House Children's Books,
61–63 Uxbridge Road, London W5 5SA

www.kidsatrandomhouse.co.uk

Addresses for companies within The Random House Group Limited can be found at:
www.randomhouse.co.uk/offices.htm

THE RANDOM HOUSE GROUP Limited Reg. No. 954009

A CIP catalogue record for this book is available from the British Library.

Printed in China